BUKAYO SAKA

Incredible Football Stories

PLAYER OF THE MONTH

FOOTBALL SERIES

DREAM SUPERSTAR

KIMI KANE

this Book Belongs to

_____

_____

_____

Once upon a time, there was a boy who loved football and basketball. He also loved acting. He loved these three things so much that he was always involved in one of them at every point in time.

He was asked in one of his interviews what profession he would have chosen if he wasn't a footballer. He said he would have been a basketballer or an actor. He said he grew up watching Will Smith and his favorite show was the French Prince of Bel-Air.

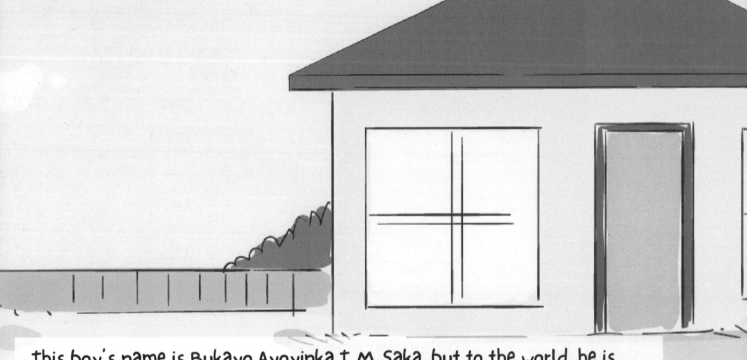

this boy's name is Bukayo Ayoyinka T.M Saka, but to the world, he is known as Saka or Little Chilli. He got the nickname from his captain Pie Emerick Aubameyang.
Bukayo Saka said they were doing one finishing drill in training and he kept scoring. He said he was shooting with so much power and he could hear Aubameyang calling him Little Chilli. He said that was how the name stuck.

Bukayo Ayoyinka Saka was born on the 5th of September 2001 to Nigerian parents in the city of London. His parents were immigrants who before he was born left Nigeria to settle in London in search of better living and more opportunities.

Bukayo Ayoyinka Saka was born on the 5th of September 2001 to Nigerian parents in the city of London. His parents were immigrants who before he was born left Nigeria to settle in London in search of better living and more opportunities.

Bukayo Saka's parents were passionate football lovers. Their love for football and the desire to change their social status made them consider the possibility of taking their child to a football academy.

Since both parents were Arsenal fans, it was normal that they will choose Arsenal's academy for Bukayo Saka.

Arsenal Football academy is one of the best in England, therefore, the application was reserved for the best young footballers. Because his parents know how extremely talented their kid was, they didn't hesitate to apply.

the trial came and Bukayo Saka passed in flying colors. At this time, the pride of his parent and his family members knew no bounds.

After passing the trial, Bukayo Saka joined Arsenal's Hale End academy at the age of seven. His early days at the academy weren't easy. Saka and his parent made a lot of sacrifices to ensure his continued stay at the academy

In one of Bukayo Saka's interviews about his time at the academy, Bukayo Saka said "It was quite a struggle for my parents to help me get here, but they always gave their all and got me into training".

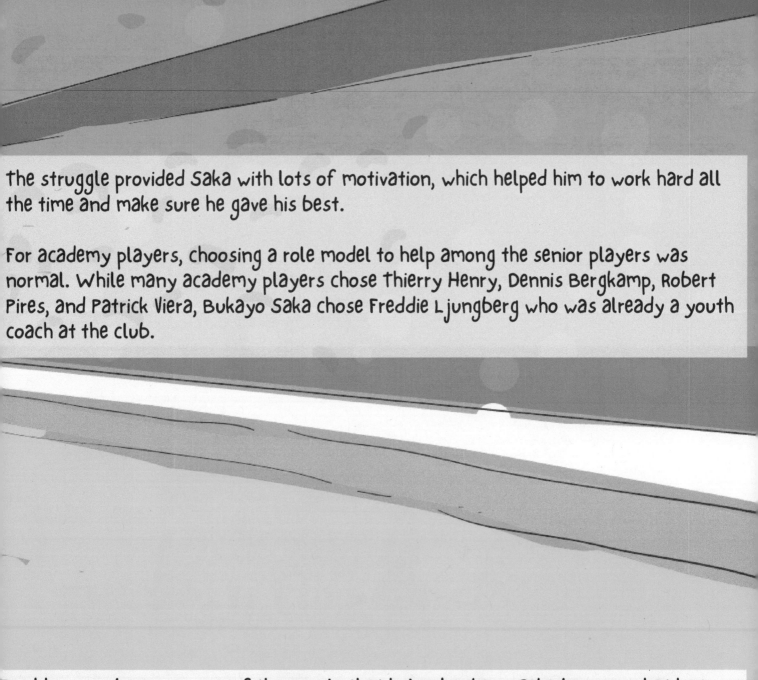

the struggle provided Saka with lots of motivation, which helped him to work hard all the time and make sure he gave his best.

For academy players, choosing a role model to help among the senior players was normal. While many academy players chose Thierry Henry, Dennis Bergkamp, Robert Pires, and Patrick Viera, Bukayo Saka chose Freddie Ljungberg who was already a youth coach at the club.

Freddie Ljungberg was one of the people that helped Bukayo Saka become what he is today. He helped Bukayo Saka remain humble and made him work extra hard in training. After coaching Bukayo Saka for a few years, Freddie Ljungberg predicted that Bukayo Saka was going to be a top player for the club and the national team.

As days went by, people began to notice Bukayo Saka.

As soon as Bukayo Saka clocked 17 years, he was given a professional contract and was promoted to the U-23 side.

After a series of impressive performances with the U-23 side, he was promoted to the first team.

On the 19th of November 2018, Bukayo Saka made his derby for the senior team in a Europa League match against Vorskla Poltava. He came on as a substitute for Aaron Ramsey in the 68th minute.

On the 13th of December 2018, Bukayo Saka made his full home debut for Arsenal in their Europa League match against Qarabag.

On the 1st of January 2019, Bukayo Saka made his Premier League debut in a 4-1 win against Fulham Football Club when he came on for Alex Iwobi in the 83rd minute. He became the first player born in the 21st century to play in a Premier League match

Bukayo Saka scored his first senior goal on the 19th of September 2019 in a 3-0 win against Eintracht Frankfurt in the Europa League. His performance in that match earned him his first premier league against Aston Villa that weekend. He then registered an assist for Pierre Emerick Aubameyang, setting up an equalizer in a 1-1 draw against Manchester United at Old Trafford.

At 18 years and 125 days old, Bukayo Saka became the youngest player starter in Premier League history to start Manchester United versus Arsenal clash.

Bukayo Saka continued to churn out good performances and on the 1st of July 2020, he was awarded a new long-term contract. At the unveiling of Bukayo Saka's new contract, Arsenal Head coach Mikel Arteta said "I think Saka represents every value that this football club stands for. He has come through the academy and earned his respect with hard work and accountability and you can see the progression that he is having as a player as well as a person.

He helped Arsenal win the F.A cup trophy that season. He was voted as the third-best Arsenal player of the season. Bukayo Saka started the 2020/2021 season very strong. He was named in the starting eleven against Liverpool in the community shield. He helped Arsenal win the community shield.

On the 26th of December 2020, he scored his third Premier League goal against Chelsea. He was later voted player of the Month on Arsenal's official website for December and January. He finished the season with seven goals and seven assists and he was voted Arsenal player of the season.

Bukayo Saka started the 2021/2022 season very well.

He was voted Arsenal player of the season for the second time in a row, becoming the first player to retain the award after Thierry Henry in 2004.

Bukayo Saka is single as several investigations have shown. Maybe he prefers to focus on his football rather than looking for a girlfriend.

He is a Christian. Saka does not have a specific goal celebration. Sometimes he takes off his shirt when he scores a goal. Sometimes, he celebrates his goal by running across the pitch or hugging his teammates.

Get Free Coloring Activity Pages

https://qimi.co/football